Clever Mr Beaver

&

the

Baby Dragon That Ran Out of Puff

by

Spike Brown

Illustrated by

Karl Whiteley

Tower Bridge Books

Copyright © Spike Brown

Illustrations © Karl Whiteley 2024

Spike Brown has asserted his right under the copyright, designs and patents act of 1988 to be identified as the author of this book.

All rights reserved.

No part of this publication may be reproduced, stored in a retrieval system, or transmitted in any form or by any means, electronic, mechanical, photocopying, recording or otherwise, without the prior permission of the copyright owner.

A catalogue record of this book is available from the British Library

Contents

For Julie

Animal Rescue

Just imagine… three cottages in a row, tucked away within the small hamlet of Ark Rise. Some three country miles distant from Toad Hall. The middle cottage inhabited by old plough horses Jane and Horace Clomper, both retired agricultural workers. At one end the Peckham's, with their substantial chicken brood. The other end, Ma Porksley and her sweet little piglets Kate, Bella and Timmy – **never mind the bleak, bitter weather, the ice and the snow.**

Yes - horses, piggy's and chickens prepared to come out of doors and pitch in, all the animals helping each other with one shared goal – to get a baby dragon to come down from the roof safely and as Jane Clomper remarked, 'For he seemed to them severely out of puff, in need of firing up, to getting that flaming breath going again'.

A long-time resident of Ark Rise, t'was Horace Clomper, who earlier that afternoon came out to lay a bucket of fireplace cinders on the snowy path, only to hear a faint mewling noise from up on next doors roof, which made him step back and glance up – 'blow me!' if it wasn't a **baby dragon**, desperate for warmth, leaning against the chimney pot shivering away.

Stuck! Up there on the tiles!

Fortunately, far from being dumb, Mr Clomper, a wise old equine, sent word immediately to the police house. Which was some quarter of a mile distant from Ark Rise.

Despite snow flurries and deep drifts, the officer arrived promptly on his bicycle to assess the scene. His first task being to phone his superiors from the nearby police

box: "Notify – a baby dragon in distress - stuck on roof -
Send assistance - post haste'

Beaver Sprays Cologne

This still being the Christmas holiday, Mr Toad of Toad Hall, the local squire and major landowner in those parts, certainly acquainted with the hamlet of Ark rise and its spartan populace (through collection of rent by his estate manager), must also be informed – **the sudden**

appearance of a baby dragon (being as any naturalist would tell us – a species long extinct) sure to excite his clever curiosity.

Meanwhile, the rescue effort commenced with due diligence, nothing rash though – for one thing, Sgt Clayburn noticed Horace Clomper crouching down, about to haul a set of ladders from over by the wall. The sergeant of police was having none of that.

"**No ladders by order** 'ole son. **Safety first** – we don't want no heroics Mr Clomper, fine gesture, but yer wife w'ont appreciate you climbin' up, losing yer hoofin' an slippin' orf the roof guttering in the slippery snow and doing 'yerself a mischief. Best we coax the little critter down somehow!"

"Fire's wot dragons like aint it?" Squealed Ma Porksley from over the garden wall, "To my way of thinking it all boils down to mother's milk, why, if it likes fire, then let the baby have plenty."

"Well, for goodness's sake, **let's light a brazier then**," Proposed Ena Peckham from the upstairs window of No.1, showing off her fancy new 'hairdo'.

"Atta gal," Came the warm response of the neighbour's, all animals dead keen on the rescue effort.

"A contained fire might well be the best way forward – attract it 'orf the roof." Agreed Sgt Clayburn, scanning the chimney pots with focused eyes.

A rooster that was never short of bright ideas, Mr Fred Peckham proposed the following – "Naw, me missus swears by **Hogwarts perifinalium**, tha' old country cure's the answer," he chipped in. "Tha's a field of it growing nearby, rightly steep in warm, fermented ginger beer, it acts as a tonic see. Poor little spikey fella." He clucked; "E' needs a good old pick-me-up, so he does."

"Maybe, but for now we need a good fire Fred, proper coal flames, that'd be best. I'll go fetch a brazier from the shed." Old Horace the horse gamely trotted back indoors,

giving his wife a cheeky little wink. She waggled her long eyelashes, with a warm smile demurely in response.

Up above, baby dragon was aware, it understood, for it was now moving its scaly little head this a way and that a way in hope.

Good heavens, then it started to edge itself timidly away from the brick chimney base, using it's forked tail as a counterbalance.

The dragon baring its scratchy-screechy claws, virtually **skated down the frozen slates**, only to end up teetering on the edge of the icicle encrusted roof guttering.

This latest move was greeted by gasps of astonishment from down below. Would the guttering hold its weight? For as we all know, a dragon no matter large or small is heavy with muscle and dense bone structure.

"C'mon spikey, w'ell catch yer if you fall," cried one of the piglets from the end cottage.

Timmy decided he must do something, but what exactly? He searched his weeny brain, and for his age group came up with a tolerably good solution!

"My tadpole net – we'll catch baby in my tadpole net!" He was poised to fetch it from the shed out back.

Bella, his older sister, was dismissive, "no Timmy, that's silly. **A tadpole net won't be strong enough**. Mummy should we gather a pile of straw to break its fall?"

"Wait! Listen. You young 'ns mark my words," said Sgt Clayburn, helping Horace set up the tripod legs on which to mount the fire basket. "Brazier'll do the trick, some say dragons find fire irresistible – so catch E's eye see, get 'im interested, flap straight down for them burnin' coals E' will."

"Oh, do look," clucked Mrs Peckham, craning her crop, as she leaned further out of the upstairs window, getting a (chicken's) bird's eye view of proceedings. **"Baby's livening up it is, cluck, cluck."**

Indeed, it was, perched up there on the cottage roof, baby dragon took a keen interest, watching while Horace the horse piled the brazier full of kindling, stuffing in balls of crumpled newspaper, then a couple of shovel fulls of coal. When the thing was done, the whole lot set light by way of a swiftly struck match.

A fiery blaze soon got flaming.

A good fry up

The Plot Thickens

The honking of a motor car's horn heralded the arrival outside the row of cottages, of a Morris traveller, driven by old Shire horse Alan Plumly, the canny manager of a posh care home for the rich and elderly.

Also, sat in the rear, were a couple of nurses, so if needs be, medical back up was close at hand.

Soon after a black, Lanchester police patrol car, driven by **WPC Luna Thoroughgood** (bell clanging on the radiator grill) pulled up.

Out got Inspector Jack Russell, tugging on one of his floppy ears, looking very smart in his neatly pressed uniform. Also, Mr Beaver, a concerned party, accompanied by his friend Mr Badger from The Wildwood.

During a conversation with Ma Porksley in which Mr Beaver shed light on the situation, the following information emerged.

Firstly - the baby dragon had apparently, on Christmas day, escaped up and out of the staff room chimney of Tudor Close Residential Care Home. After being found initially curled up within the burning coal of the fireplace there.

Secondly – various shell fragments representative of a newly hatched (extraordinarily sized) egg, of a reddish hue, plus ripped apart Christmas wrapping paper was found outside in the corridor – **thus, the mythical became reality,** a creature of legend, a proper conundrum indeed!

But let us continue this real-life drama.

One of the nurses, Miss Guernsey, showing a very becoming pair of horns, came forward suggesting quite seriously, that the dragon, being a newborn baby **had flown the nest too early** as it were. Instead of allowing for a period of incubation.

Moley at home

In general conversation, Mr Beaver, a rather clever animal it must be said, remarked astutely that once outside in the open air, the sharp bitter winter chill, the cold, heavy atmosphere meant that the baby dragon never really attained altitude and simply **ran out of puff**. Expending all its energy flapping its wings.

Crucial to its inability to cover any long distances, hence considerably out of puff, the dragon made it only as far as Ark Rise, many miles from its intended destination. Which was, purely on primal instinct (as like a homing pigeon), a nice cave in the Black Mountains of Wales, some small distance from the capital city, Cardiff. Where it must be supposed (by pure speculation of course) legend had it that a kindly, devoted dragon family named the Ponthircaerleon's lived (undisturbed by armour clad, sword wielding man for many centuries) and who knows, should perhaps be prepared to adopt it?

Meanwhile, back at chimney pot level, baby dragon was steadily growing more and more determined, **eyes big as**

saucers, ready to launch itself directly at the burning brazier from up on the roof of Ark Rise Cottage No.1.

The girls, resourceful as always had managed to quickly assemble the ladder and prop it up against the house front – Daisy Buttercup climbed up to get a closer view, while Nurse Guernsey held the ladder steady.

Beating its wings frantically, flap flapperty, flap flapperty, flap flap! Shockingly it quite suddenly took off – an airborne baby dragon! Steeped in the slow pace of rural life, the seasons, the agricultural landscape, the harvest home – nobody in Ark Rise had ever seen anything quite like it at all. The assembled cottage residents held their collective breath. Hooves, claws and trotters all well crossed for good luck as, with a mixture of frantic flapping and instinctual confidence in its abilities, the dragon launched off.

But had it worked…?

How sparks flew that winters evening – where once down and nestled amongst the red-hot crackly coals of the brazier, the baby dragon seemed to perk up and gain a modicum of strength.

All the animals of Ark Rise were delighted. But Mr Beaver and Mr Badger, both hefty chaps, wisely kept them all at a distance with arms spread out as a barrier. Curbing the younger members with their tendency to inquisitively push forward to get a better look of the baby and possibly topple the brazier.

Alas, it soon became apparent that the fire seemed insubstantial, **the dragon's skin pallor remained decidedly pale and grey**. Snuffling from a heavy cold, eyelids drooping, emitting only spasmodic rasps of thin vapour, no real smoke to talk of (apart from that coming from the brazier).

"A bonfire! Quickly!" Directed Mr Beaver. "We must build a big bonfire – c'mon you fellas, get cracking, more flames, **the hotter the better.**"

He, and old Badger, hurried about with the others collecting anything burnable from the gardens – the Peckham's brought out sticks of furniture, Ma Porksley fetched bits of old carpet, straw and wot not from the cellar. A bonfire pyramid being hastily assembled by Horace and Jane.

Mr Toad Takes Control

The generosity and many kindnesses of the rural poor, never failed to rouse in Mr Toad feelings of affection towards his tenants.

Motoring into the small hamlet that afternoon, he was

fascinated to see a bonfire burning in one of the gardens. Animal folk huddled round, not (he judged so much) from the freezing cold, more snow being forecast, but with a desperately sad expression upon their firelit furry and feathery features.

Our most amiable squire recognised Sgt Clayburn, also the very pucker Inspector Jack Russell from the local rural force. There too, were his best chums, dear old Badger and Mr Beaver, the professional dam engineer responsible for the 'riverbank flood prevention scheme' that had successfully seen flood levels reduced in the area, therefore protecting property from water damage. His other talent was for solving crime, but dear **oh dear, something was wrong.**

Normally jovial, easy-going fellows they too looked so concerned – why such long faces for heaven's sake? It was Christmas holiday.

He parked his yellow Rolls Royce, allowing friends Moley and Ratty to further investigate, for the eager animals jumped out of the car and ran towards the fiery scene. On a winter's afternoon, temperatures dipping, a bonfire seemed to be of sound sense.

"What's up?" The squire wearing plus fours, a very fine full length, fur collared overcoat, screwing in his monocle, strode purposefully toward the gathered crowd – he, the most handsome and equitable Toad alive had not long to wait for an answer – quickly, he realised the reason for the glum aspects upon faces, for **curled up in the heart of the flames of the roaring bonfire, a dragon lay panting,** its breathing shallow, its normally bright green prickly skin sallow and grey.

The most senior policeman on scene stepped forward. "The incident is ongoing and concerns a baby dragon Sir."

Said Inspector Russell, saluting Mr Toad, "We're doing all we can, but it's very poorly – two nurses are in attendance as we speak."

"Blasted shame," exclaimed Mr Beaver walking over, shaking paws warmly with Mr Toad, "Only a baby see – none of us know what to do, we just can't seem to get it right."

Hurrying across to update the squire, holding onto her prim white nurse's cap, Daisy Buttercup further elaborated. "Oh, Mr Toad, no matter how much heat and flame, even from that sizeable bonfire – **the baby dragon just isn't responding** – looks like it's wilting away, we think he flew the nest much too early you see, and flying in cold temperatures seems to have done for the poor little mite – needs to incubate it does, to settle its metabolism. That's the chemical processes in such a living creature to enhance its growth and energy!"

"Incubate, eh?" On occasions Mr Toad could himself be very smart up top, he thought for barely half a minute, and adjusting his monocle, replied, "Metabawotsits? Hang it all, I may have just the answer." But the first priority he felt, was that it would be no bad thing to cheer everybody up a bit. **"Look 'E here, you Ark Risers – you lovely rabble of rural scallywags – chin up!** I'm invitin' y'all to a slap-up feed at Toad Hall. Horace me old fruit – be a sport an' hitch up to that wagonette of yours – plenty of room for all of you Ark Risers wot!"

Ratty reads The Times

Thereafter, Mr Toad issued further directives to both his commendable tenants and all others that were involved in the rescue.

"Wrap the little nipper up in a blanket, E' aint done for yet, not by a long chalk, not if I have anything to do with it."

Sporty Toad!

Brimming with positivity, **Toad hopped up and down**, his upbeat mood was infectious, goading all the animals to damp down the bonfire, and rush indoors for their hats and coats – after all, it wasn't every day that you got invited into the manor. Horace Clomper brought round the wagonette, and everyone clambered on board, his wife Jane atop of the box seat. Ena and Fred Peckham and their brood clucking merrily, Ma Porksley and her eager little piglets Kate, Bella and Timmy wriggling excitedly on the wagon bench, **"Off to the 'big house'! How grand, ooh, the grub must be yummy there I'll bet!"**

After conferring with his pals Mr Badger and Beaver, who would share the Rolls with Ratty and Mole on the way back.

Toad took a ginormous leap into the air, ending up plonked behind the wheel of his sleek motor.

With a **beep-beep-beep** the procession of vehicles rumbled up the country lane in search of Toad Hall, the rural hamlet of Ark Rise soon left behind.

Wheels crunched on a road surface comprising of early morning snow fall, now crisply frozen in heaps. The arable land thereabouts at this season was but a white mass divided by hedgerows and dry-stone walling, visible were the occasional farmhouse, with barns and groups of out buildings.

Toad's yellow convertible was tailed by the black Lanchester patrol car with Sgt Clayburn clanging the radiators emergency bell by means of a string, Alan Plumly's nippy Morris Traveller and last but by no means least, trotting along at a fair old rate was Horace Clomper, drawing his wagon load of lively Ark Risers.

Barely conscious, but thankfully still alive, baby dragon was hugged close to the bosom of nurse Guernsey, who licked her long tongue tenderly about the scaly, cute, little face that was **swaddled up in blankets.**

A Plan is Hatched

Later that afternoon Mr Tolly, the general handyman, part gardener and one of the more prominent staff members at the manor, was summoned from the cottage that he shared with his wife on the estate.

Intrigued, for Mr Toad on the wind-up inter-staff telecommunication system requested that he straight away head out into the cold, and over to the engine shed to fire up Mirabelle, the little garden locomotive that had more than earned its keep every summer, by taking children and guests round the grounds.

MIRABELLE, a stroke of unmitigated genius. Toady had risen to the challenge once again alright. How fortunate the master of Toad Hall chose to invest in the garden railway.

All the animal folk were ushered by servants to that same place, with a promise of a slap-up tea, to be served later in the banqueting hall – this only after a certain very serious matter could be resolved.

Mr Badger, dressed in practical country tweeds and broad shouldered, squat Mr Beaver, the marine mammal, sporting his deer stalker, pipe tucked into the corner of his mouth, strode ahead with Lord of the manor Mr Toad - Ratty and Mole all in fine fettle, keen to know what exactly their esteemed friend was up to.

The word **incubate** had been banded around in the car earlier on.

Nurse Guernsey hurried across the grounds; a swathed bundle carried limply in her arms. Alas, **her patient was**

weakening – neither she nor Daisy Buttercup held out much hope, **they honestly didn't think baby would make it!**

The cold, harsh, wintry weather held out little sympathy either, it appeared eager to quell, to stamp out any upstart firebreather.

Old bespectacled Horace the horse, the retired farmworker was first to notice a good deal of smoke belching out from a chimney over by the corrugated iron and brick built shed, situated to one side of the stable block. **Why, how he beamed**, his muzzle drew back into a wide toothy grin, revealing bright pink gums. Jane his wife, flicking back her fringe, understood at once, for at heart her husband was a **'steam nut'** who loved anything to do with the railways. He used to like nothing better than hauling a cart load of swedes to the country station so he could watch the trains puff by. Owning a rather splendid clockwork, tabletop, model railway up in the attic.

So, there it was, the animals, the fowls of Ark Rise and everyone else gathered round. The whole crowd now had an inkling of what lay afoot – **the clues were all there** – a tiny maroon and blue steam loco, suitable for a garden track was being fired up, lumps of old pallet wood and black Welsh coal being shovelled into the firebox. **A real nice blaze going.**

The brass pressure gauge moving up into the red.

A chap in cap and overalls sat astride of the tender, fully intent on his job.

Given responsibility for the baby dragon – no sooner did Mr Tolly cradle the little creature gently in his strong steady hands, somehow all present knew that there would be a happy ending – **baby's eyes filled with warmth and comfort** as an audible, satisfied mewling sound surfaced from between its jaws.

It sensed the basking, internal heat of the gorgeous firebox close by.

Under the nurse's supervision, **baby dragon was laid carefully into the flames,** the furnace door shut firmly with a clang.

A promise made to Mr Toad, that for the next few days the engines fire should be constantly maintained, Mirabelle should act as the baby's incubator, coal was to be shovelled in at intervals both day and night, never allowing the flames to damp down – maximum heat deployed. Mr Tolly's wife Dora was fully trained up as a railway footplate crew member, so she could assist. Which she willingly and ably did.

What a banquet progressed that evening at Toad Hall — **after a sumptuous feast,** Fred Peckham took up his harmonica (which he kept in his inside pocket at all times) and **everyone clapped and danced,** twirling each other round in a glorious barn dance to such favourite tunes as 'Tis the First of May, She'll Be Coming Round The Mountain and Roger De Coverly!

A magnanimous time was had by all, and **toast upon toast was presented to the squire** for his clever and kind initiative. For let's be clear here, Mr Toad on occasion could be a very smart toad indeed, even clever Mr Beaver took his hat off to him that night.

As a footnote...

...Early one morning (on the third day), Tolly and his coal smudged wife in their filthy engineman's caps and overalls, each having taken a shift over at the engine shed, were preparing a hurried hearty breakfast, when gazing out of the kitchen window they both beheld **smoke writing, puffily drifting above the horizon –**

The manor house was also stirring, Mr Toad enjoying his morning coffee and newspaper in front of a large window in the oak panelled dining hall, saw the same.

He could only draw one conclusion, that **BABY DRAGON WAS FULL OF PUFF**, and now off on his way.

Which proved to be the case.

Enjoying his morning coffee

Many at Ark Rise and along the riverbank beyond were also witness to this sky writing event. An event that would be talked about for many years after.

Mr Toad's
Die Cast Model Cars™

Mr Toad's Toy Cars. You too can live the high life, just like Mr Toad!
With the Totally new collection of 1:76 scale die cast model cars.

Drive down country lanes in the yellow roller!

Do a loop of the grounds on Mirabelle!

Take a ride in the Morris Traveller!

Respond! In the Police force Lanchester Tourer.

For one car only , send 3' shilling to the address below.
For all for send £1.00 to the address below
(do not forget to let us know which model you would like & send a return address)
Toad's Toys, Toad Hall, West of Wildwood, North of River SP17 3WW

Clever Mr Beaver supports:

Please Donate

www.hillside.org.uk

Hillside Animal Sanctuary

Hall Lane, Frettenham,

Norwich, NR12 7LT

www.ingramcontent.com/pod-product-compliance
Lightning Source LLC
Chambersburg PA
CBHW061225210726
48294CB00006B/1979